THE BEST MARIACHI IN THE WORLD

El mejor mariachi del mundo

Written by / Escrito por
J.D. Smith
Illustrated by / Ilustrado por
Dani Jones

For all the Gustavos of the world,
and for one very special Magaly. —JDS

For Nik and Shan. — DJ

Text Copyright © 2008 J.D. Smith
Illustration Copyright © Dani Jones
Translation Copyright © 2008 Raven Tree Press

All rights reserved. For information about permission to reproduce selections from this book, write to: Raven Tree Press, A Division of Delta Systems Co., Inc., 1400 Miller Parkway, McHenry, IL 60050 www.raventreepress.com

Smith, J.D.

The Best Mariachi in the World / written by J.D. Smith; illustrated by Dani Jones; translated by Eida de la Vega = El mejor mariachi del mundo / escrito por J.D. Smith; ilustrado por Dani Jones; traducción al español de Eida de la Vega. – 1 ed. – McHenry, IL ; Raven Tree Press, 2008.

p.:cm.

Bilingual Edition
ISBN 978-09770906-1-7 hardcover
ISBN 978-09794462-4-5 paperback

English Edition
ISBN 978-1887744-99-7 hardcover
ISBN 978-1887744-98-0 paperback

Spanish Edition
ISBN 978-1887744-97-3 hardcover
ISBN 978-1887744-96-6 paperback

SUMMARY: Gustavo wants to be in the family mariachi band, but he cannot play the violines, trompetas or guitarrones. He finds his place in the band with his singing talent.

Audience: Pre–K to 3rd grade.
Bilingual—with mostly English story and concept words in Spanish, English–only and Spanish–only formats.

1. Ethnic Hispanic & Latino—Juvenile fiction. 2. Bilingual books.
3. Picture books for children. 4. Spanish language materials—Bilingual.
I. Illus. Dani Jones. II. Title. III. El mejor mariachi del mundo.

Library of Congress Control Number 2008920929

Printed in Taiwan
10 9 8 7 6 5 4 3 2 1
first edition

The Best MARIACHI in the World

El mejor mariachi del mundo

Written by / Escrito por J.D. Smith
Illustrated by / Ilustrado por Dani Jones

Raven Tree Press
A Division of Delta Systems Co., Inc.
www.raventreepress.com

Gustavo was the worst **mariachi** in the world. Everyone else in the family band could play an instrument. But not Gustavo. He did not play songs at weddings or at restaurants. He did not wear **un traje de charro** or **un sombrero**.

Sometimes he reached for the bow of his brother Raymundo's violin. Raymundo quietly said, "Don't touch the bow of my **violín**. You might break it. It is not for you."

Sometimes Gustavo tried to play his Uncle Enrique's brass trumpet. Uncle Enrique gently said, "Put down **la trompeta**. You might drop it. It is not for you."

Gustavo did not even try to pick up his father's **guitarrón**. It was taller than he was.

Gustavo wondered how it would feel to strum the long strings, the long **cuerdas**. He imagined everyone would listen. People would look at him. The men and women would get up and dance. All the children would dance and clap.

He would be Gustavo, the great **mariachi**.

But that would never happen. No one would let him play. He would always be the worst **mariachi** in the world.

Even his cousins would not let him try to play their **guitarrón,** or **tocar una trompeta** or **violín.**

They would say, "This is not for you."

"Hmm," Gustavo thought, "I want to be in the band—in **la banda mariachi.** But what can I do?"

Gustavo got up one morning before dawn. He looked out into the desert and saw the cacti. The saguaros stood like huge trees. The nopales lay close to the ground. The sky was a black bowl of stars. Somewhere an owl hooted. A coyote padded over the sand. Everything was beautiful.

No one was there to play. But he had to stand up and sing. He just had to **cantar**.

He sang softly at first, barely moving his lips.

The next day he got up a little earlier. He sang in a whisper.

The day after that Gustavo **cantó** a little bit louder.

14

The following day he sang louder still. He did not think about where he was or how early it was.

Before the first rooster crowed, before the first light of day peeked out from the east, Gustavo sang, and **cantó** at the top of his voice.

One by one, the lights in the houses came on.

A man called out, "What is happening?"

A woman wondered, "Who is that?"

A child asked, "Who is that **cantante**?"

Gustavo kept singing.

He sang of traveling men. He sang of faraway places and of coming home again.

He sang all the songs he knew. He sang all **las canciones** that he knew like his own name.

A crowd of people came out to listen.

At last Gustavo finished singing. He was done with his **canciones**. He turned to go inside. It was time to feed the chickens.

The people started to clap. They liked his singing! They were clapping for **su canto**.

"Gustavo!" they called out. "**¡Bravo! ¡Muy bueno!**"

They kept clapping. Women waved their handkerchiefs.

His brother gave him a big hug and said, "You are a real **mariachi.**"

His father said, "You, my son, just may be the best **mariachi** in the world."

His cousins carried Gustavo, the best **mariachi**, into the house. They made him a huge breakfast. Then they fed the chickens for him.

The next time the band played, Gustavo wore **un traje de charro**. He wore **un sombrero**. He sang **las canciones** that had brought everyone outside.

All the people clapped and cheered. He took off his **sombrero** and took a deep bow.

"This," Gustavo thought, "is for me."

Vocabulary / Vocabulario

English	Español
violin	el violín
trumpet	la trompeta
guitar	la guitarra /el guitarrón
dance	bailar
sing	cantar /cantó
band	la banda
singer	el cantante
song	la canción
sombrero	el sombrero
charro suit	el traje de charro

Mariachis have been playing music since about 1880. Some people believe the name mariachi was a kind of tree used to make stages and musical instruments that mariachis play. Most mariachi bands have the Spanish guitar (guitarra), a bass guitar with a rounded back (guitarrón), a high–pitched guitar with five strings (vihuela), violins, and at least two trumpets.